MARY & GOD

Jon Ferguson

Huge Jam Publishing, 2022
www.hugejam.com

DEDICATION

To my children — Jackson, Fanny, and Jodie —
and lovers of life everywhere.

AUTHOR'S NOTE

To understand this book one must be able to swim outside the fishbowl of Western thinking wherein ideas about the origin of the world, life, god, virgin birth, Jesus, Mary, truth, teleology, theology, ontology, free will, time, space, etc. are pretty much universally tattooed on our brains. The best example I can think of is that 99.99% of Westerners believe that the world had a beginning and that that beginning was either a creation by God (the so-called "Judeo-Christian" one) or something called "The Big Bang". People cannot even fathom another possibility, such as, for example, that there was no beginning… that everything always was, is, and will be… that it is simply always changing.

Another example of the tattoos on our brains is the idea that man is somehow separate from nature. The Platonic hierarchy of God-Man-Animal-Plant-Rock, etc. – with nature being everything that comes below man – is essentially ubiquitous.

I have spent the greater part of my sixty-three years on earth trying to erase these tattoos in an effort to see the world for what it really is. Of course this might be an impossible task. Of course I might be wasting my time. Of course "truth" might be an absurd notion, a man-made concept that has nothing to do with anything.

This book is the sequel to Jesus & Mary. The last paragraph of that book is the first paragraph of this book. Both are love stories. When all is said and done, maybe love is the only thing that can stick to the ribs of mankind.

ONE

Night was coming. The moment Jesus expired, Mary was the only person at the foot of the cross. Paul and the others had left hours before when their friend had stopped talking. Mary lay on her back and stared at the same sky Jesus had looked at that morning as he was being attached to the two wooden planks. As the heavens darkened a few scattered stars were beginning to twinkle. Mary had brought the tattered blanket that she and Jesus had slept under for the last three years. She curled her body inside it placing both hands on her slightly inflated belly. Before she was asleep, one hand crawled out to wipe away the few final drops of blood that fell on the face that the dead man on the cross had so adored.

TWO

Two months before Jesus's barbaric crucifixion, he and Mary Magdalene had made love like no two people had done before. Why? Simply because no two humans had ever loved each other as much as Jesus and Mary loved. They were the real Adam and Eve. Each adored every aspect of the other's being. Each respected every moment of the other's life. Each constantly felt the miracle of being alive. It was easier for Jesus to love than Mary, because he had been given love as a boy. He knew what love was when he was a child. Mary didn't. She had none growing up. She had been an orphan and had had to fend for herself. She was actually stronger than Jesus. She had to invent love. She had to turn hell into heaven. She had to rise above the coldness of the world and learn to love. Jesus just took the love he had received as a child, expanded it, and spread it around. Mary had to rewrite the script of her life. That happened when she met Jesus. Love became a real possibility. Love was no longer a foreign country. The most important thing was that little by little she began to realize that Jesus really did love her. She slowly but surely began to love herself. The more she loved herself, the more she loved Jesus. And the more she loved Jesus, the more Jesus loved her. The more Jesus loved her, the more she loved Jesus. They fused. When they made love there was no separation. Eventually they were always making love, even when apart.

So two months before Jesus was nailed to the cross, Mary became pregnant. Seven months after his absurd death she gave birth to a boy. They had decided to name him "God" – God Magdalene Christ. He was born in the home Jesus's father had built, the same home where Jesus and Mary had lived for three wonderful years before his murder, for murder it was by the powers that were in place more than two thousand years ago in the area around Jerusalem.

Though fatherless, God had a wonderful childhood. Mary loved him like she had loved Jesus. And Mary taught him to love the world in return. She taught him to appreciate everything, especially being alive. She instilled in God a feeling for the mystery of life, all life. As a child God would look at his hands and wonder where the five fingers came from — and why five and not three or twelve? He would breathe and feel the air rush in and out of his nose and throat, and when he would exhale he would put his hand in front of his mouth and the air would tickle his skin. Sometimes when Mary would talk to him he would put a finger in each ear and her voice would disappear. How did these ears work? How did sounds form in his mother's mouth and travel into his ears? And when he would put bread into his mouth, he would realize that his mouth and teeth would chew without thinking, as if his body knew on its own that it had to grind up the food so it could pass into his body. How could a body know what to do without a head giving it instructions? Where did thoughts and feelings come from? When he would run through the hills he wondered how his legs worked, what propelled them? Why could birds and butterflies fly, but not him and his mother Mary?

What fascinated God most were his eyes. He would close them and there was nothing except some funny patterns that seemed to sparkle a bit in the dark. But then when he would open them again there was the world he was used to. What an amazing circus of lines and colors and movement! Often he would go to the marketplace with his mother and sit for hours and watch the lines and colors dance in front of him. What a kaleidoscope! He wondered if other eyes saw the same lines and colors that he was seeing. He wondered if animal eyes saw differently than people eyes. And he asked himself if what he was seeing was "real", and maybe his eyes were "wrong" and other eyes were "right", or maybe there was no such thing as right and wrong when it came to seeing.

When God reached age twelve he had a strange feeling that his eyes always saw only the surface of things and in seeing the surface, they never got to the "reality" of anything. He wondered if and how anybody could get to the *reality*… maybe there was no *reality*…

Yes, God was a curious boy and Mary fed his curiosity. She would listen and smile and tell him how his mind so resembled that of his father. He would tell her about insects he had followed and examined — ants, beetles, and spiders. Where do they come from? How long have they been on earth? Are they happy? Do they feel pain, joy, love, hunger, fear? Do they ever get lonely? What makes them move forward? What tells them to stop? How do they get all those legs to work in unison? Are they obeying orders? Then God would ask his mother the same questions about people. Why do people do what they do? How do their bodies work? What makes an arm or a tongue or foot move...?

God had many friends as he was nice to people. He was happy; he made others happy in turn. He would smile infinitely more than he would frown. He laughed much more than he cried. Many things made him laugh, but only two things made him cry, and one of those things was joy. Sometimes he would walk through the world and be so happy that tears of joy would roll from the corners of his eyes. The other thing that made him cry was death, the death of people or animals large and small. He hated death. His mother would tell him that he had to accept it, that it was part of "life", but he still hated the thought of creatures he loved disappearing forever. "But it might not be forever," Mary would say. "But, mother" God would answer, "what if it is?"

He was, however, saddened by the fact that, except for his mother, the other people in Judea didn't care about his ideas and questions. They didn't wonder about why things were the way they were. They didn't marvel at the moon and stars, the sea, the sky, the earth and all creatures thereon. They always acted like everything was *normal* and there was no reason to ask questions about anything. When he would ask someone where everything came from or why things were this or that way, the person would just quote the Bible and say Jehovah made it all in six days. How, wondered God, could people be satisfied with such simplistic answers? How could people live with their heads in the sand? But they did, and little by little he realized that *that's just the way people were*. Little by little he learned not to expect too much from his friends and acquaintances. But also, little by little God began to feel more and more alone. The noise of the marketplace began to tire him. His friends started to bore him and he in turn bored them. There was only one friend with whom he could really talk, Joshua, who was thought to be the son of Marcus, the Roman soldier, yet there was no certainty about this given that Joshua's mother, Deborah, was said to be a harlot. "That poor boy will never know who his real father is," the Jews would to say. "When your mother is a whore, Satan is always your father."

When hair commenced to grow above and below God's lips, his thoughts about his father multiplied. Who really was this man people were sometimes calling the "Son of Jehovah"? How could he possibly have *died for the sins of the world* as certain people were murmuring? How could he have been resurrected when nothing else was "resurrected"? Why Jesus? There were plenty of other good people who were nailed to crosses by the Romans…

God did not believe what he was hearing about his father. Mary had told him that Jesus had not believed in the concept of "sin" or in the veracity of the Jewish god. So God did not believe that Jesus was the son of Jehovah any more than he thought his friend Joshua was the son of the devil.

THREE

It was the man Paul that started spreading the word about Jesus being divine. God watched Paul wander through the streets trying to get people to listen to him. Mary had told her son that Paul was a sad man, a sick man, a man who did not love the world the way Jesus had. She said the truth was that Paul hated the world. "Isn't this why he is trying to start a new religion, a religion based on *another world*, an *after*life, a *better* world, a *kingdom of God in heaven*," she said one evening when they were having supper. God knew his father never thought any of this. His father had been sure of only one thing: life on this earth, the here and now, what he could see, touch, and feel. Jesus had loved the world for what it was. He had accepted it. Of course he had wanted to try to make it *better*, but not by telling lies about another world. Jesus Christ had done what he could, but he had never preached a "Supreme Being" that had created man and the earth and who promised another life in some mysterious kingdom, where hell, fire, and damnation would be the lot of the so-called "sinners", and milk, honey, and eternal happiness would be waiting for all the good boys and girls! No, God knew that his father had never said such things. His father had never made promises he couldn't keep. His father had been a lover of the earth he walked on, not of some ethereal land of angels and devils… Jesus had talked about loving this life. Jesus had marveled at this life. The blood of the *miracle of existence* had constantly flowed through his veins. But after he died, God watched Paul turn all this inside out. He watched Paul take all the mystery out of life and start a religion based on suffering, fear, and his hate of his own flesh. He watched Paul use the horrendous image of his father agonizing on the cross as the symbol of the new *church*. He watched Paul spread the news that Jesus, Son of Jehovah, had been resurrected and had gone to heaven. Then he heard Paul tell the people that if *they too* wanted to go to heaven, they had to listen to him, Paul, the great Truth Sayer, and do what he said. It was a grand formula… a magic formula… And then, to top it all off, Paul came up with the Virgin Mary, a woman having a child without needing a man. Why? Because he, Paul, had never known the pleasures of the body. He had never had a woman who loved him. He had been jealous of

Jesus who shared the deepest love with God's mother, Mary Magdalene. Paul had to create a virgin mother, a virgin birth. Paul made virginity pure. Jesus had made love pure. His love for Mary had been the purest thing on earth.

So what happened? How did the world unfold? God's father, Jesus Christ, unwittingly became the object of a million lies and a million promises, none of which would be kept. Jesus was not the son of God; God was the son of Jesus. The so-called "Christian" religion that Paul and his friends invented has nothing to do with Jesus. It has nothing to do with God. The Old Testament and the New Testament are only testaments of the people who wrote them, people who saw the world as a wicked, evil, dirty, sinful place where the weak and the unhappy yearn for another life, another world... Can they be blamed for this? Of course not. When one is suffering one seeks a release from one's pain. This was Paul. This was the origin of Christianity.

FOUR

When God and Joshua were sixteen, they often walked and talked in the olive grove where Mary and Jesus had strolled the first day they met. One day their conversation went like this:

My parents used to come here often.

How do you know that?

My mother has told me so.

You're lucky. You know who your father is.

No, I don't. I never knew my father. I know his name and I've heard stories about him. But, I never saw him, never touched him, never talked to him… If Marcus is your father, then you are luckier than I am.

What do you mean?

You will have seen him alive. You will have been able to watch him move and hear his voice. Me, I never saw Jesus do anything.

And if Marcus is not my father?

Then you are in a situation similar to mine... You may never see the man that made you... Joshua, every situation can be turned inside out. You can always find a good side and a bad side to anything. And everybody does it in his or her own way. Look at the man Paul. He has taken my father's murder and is turning it into a religion. The world is a crazy place. It can go in so many crazy directions... Look at love. The more you love someone, the more pain you will feel when you lose the love. Even the 'possibility' of losing love is painful. If you don't love, you'll never have to endure the pain of its loss...

How do you know this? Have you loved?

No, but my mother has told me. We talk about such things all the time.

You are lucky to have a mother like you have.

And I am lucky to have a friend like you. You and my mother are really the only people I can talk to any more.

I have a mother, but we don't talk that much.

All mothers are different.

All fathers are different. Some are so different they are invisible.

Like mine...

I just wish the damn Jews would stop calling me a 'bastard'. No one likes to be called such a thing.

And no one should be called a 'bastard'. It's not your fault if you don't know who your father is. People are weak. People are dumb. They only belittle others to try to enlarge themselves. But it never works.

Ah, God is talking… I like to hear God speak.

Joshua, the Jews are simple people. They follow their Bible. They are like sheep following a shepherd. You cannot blame them.

I don't blame them. But I wish they would stop looking down on my mother and me.

People love to look down on others. It is how they elevate themselves. But all they are doing is showing how small they really are.

In the marketplace I once heard that crazy man Paul say that your father preached that no man has the right to judge another man.

That is one of the few truths Paul teaches. My mother has told me many times that my father never judged or condemned people. The problem with Paul is that he says that my father also said that the Almighty Jehovah can and will judge people… everybody! He will send some to "hell" and others to "heaven." My mother assures me that my father did not believe in the reality of an Almighty Jehovah, nor did he ever talk about heaven and hell, except how life here on earth can be both very beautiful and very ugly.

But God, Paul insists that your father was the son of Jehovah.

You being the son of Marcus is much more likely than my father being the son of Jehovah. My father's father was named Joseph and his mother was called

Mary like my mother.

Why does Paul say that your father's mother was a virgin?

He is trying to glorify my father and set him apart. Religions need "miracles" and new twists to things. Paul "twists" almost everything that ever came out of my father's mouth.

Why would your father's mother… your grandmother Mary… why would her being a virgin help to glorify your father?

That is a great question, Joshua. Paul is strange. He seems to be a very unhappy man.

What does your mother say about what Paul is doing?

She laughs. She says he is a weak deluded creature and that everything he is doing grows out of his unhappy pitiful life. Do you know that he tried to seduce my mother once?

How do you know?

She told me. She said he once came to her in the marketplace and told her that loving Jesus was stupid and a lost cause. He said that Jesus was going to die soon and that she should love him, Paul!

And after Jesus died…? Did he try again?

Many men have tried. But she has loved none of them.

She is a beautiful woman.

So is your mother, Joshua. All mothers are beautiful. Without them, nothing would exist.

Then all fathers are beautiful too. Without them, nothing would exist.

Then consider your father a beautiful man… even if you don't know who he is.

I will try.

It does no good to be unhappy about things you cannot control.

You are wise, God, as wise as a butterfly.

I doubt it. I too can be unhappy. Butterflies are never unhappy.

How do you know that?

I don't…

And it came to pass that God and Joshua continued their stroll back down the hill toward the marketplace where the herds were going about their business, where Joshua was called a bastard, and where God Magdalene Christ and his mother were both seen to be floating down a different river.

FIVE

While God was working on a pair of shoes, he started thinking about names and words: *God Magdalene Christ is as good a name as any. What is in a name anyway? How do words go from foreign sounds to common sounds? At first all words sound strange. But if you hear them enough, and say them enough, they become perfectly ordinary. Even big words like "teleology" or "hieroglyphic" can sound ordinary. Who invented the first words? Why are there different languages? Greek… Latin… Aramaic… I wonder about the word "Jehovah." The Bible says that Jehovah did this and Jehovah did that. Why isn't Jehovah named "Butterfly"? At least butterflies exist and can be seen and touched. Aren't butterflies as divine as Jehovah? The word "butterfly" is more beautiful than "Jehovah", especially in Latin. My mother taught me the word*

*when I was eight years old. My father had taught her…
"papillo" or "papillionus"… But what makes a word
beautiful or ugly anyway?* (God knew that Jehovah was
also called "God", but that depended on which
language one was speaking. In Latin it was "Deus",
which one day might sound like a score in a tennis
game…) *Why are people who speak a language well
or in a certain way considered more intelligent than
people who don't speak that way. What do words have
to do with intelligence? Butterflies don't talk and they
do all kinds of intelligent things. Perhaps my mother
and I don't speak the way so-called "intelligent"
people speak, but…*

God's mind wandered, but his shoes were well
made and popular. Even the Roman soldiers bought
them. Joshua's might-be father, Marcus, was the first
one to buy a pair of God's shoes and he told his friends
about them. Of course they were really more like
sandals than shoes, but what difference did that make?
They were comfortable and kept rocks and splinters
from cutting one's feet.

SIX

The days and nights of God's life had become many. Thousands and thousands had passed. The sun – O what a mystery it was! It came and went. But what was it? How big was it? How far away was it? What was it made of? Why did it change size and color? Why was it orange or red? Why was it never cut in half high in the sky like the moon? Was it the sun that made the days warm or cold? What caused the temperature of the world to change? Did the sun warm it and the moon cool it? But sometimes the days were cool and the nights were warm... God and Mary talked as they ate their bread and drank their wine at the table Jesus had made. She was now well over thirty, but still as beautiful as ever. God was tall and strong and beautiful like Jesus had been. Mary's memories of her great love were as solid and poignant as ever. She had never met another man like Jesus. A hole had been carved in her heart where Jesus lived every day, warm and safe like a mouse in a hole in the ground. One might imagine that she would have fallen in love with God. He moved like his father, had lips that cast the same silhouette, and even gave off the same odor. But Mary couldn't *fall* in love with God, because she was in love with him from the moment he existed, even when he was but a fetus in her womb. Jesus had made that baby with her. How could she not love it? But of course God-the-fetus, God-the-baby, God-the-child, and God-the-full-grown-sixteen-year-old were all different Gods. Mary often thought about how she had had to learn to love herself, and how in this world self-love is such a daunting task. How much more human time and effort is spent making people feel bad about themselves than good! How much more criticism and negative comparison there is compared to compliments and positive comparison! The Jews and Paul only drive the nails of self-dislike deeper into defenseless human hearts! We are sinful! Our bodies are sinful! Our hearts are impure! We are evil and corrupt! Only the soul is pure! What soul? The one that will float to heaven when the trials and tribulations of this life are finally over! Yes Mary Magdalene, you had to learn to love yourself, but didn't have to learn to love God. Your love for him was built into the fabric of the universe. You made God when you and Jesus were at the zenith of love, here. Jesus knew how to love.

He knew love was the only remedy for the unknown, for the mystery, for the chaos, for the pain and suffering on this earth… and for death! Wasn't death the greatest mystery of all? No! cried Jesus. Love is the greatest mystery of all. For only love can conquer death! That was the real message of Jesus: Love first; die later…!

Mary's mind often flew back to Jesus when she and God talked.

You know God, Mary said, your father even loved animals and plants. He often said, 'They are part of life, too. Why should they be of less value than anything else?'

Not many people think like that.

No, they don't. The Jews say Jehovah created plants and animals so man could eat. Jesus would laugh at that idea and say, 'Maybe Jehovah intended it to be the other way around – that animals should feed on men!'

Who knows?

Just know that your father respected it all. He could do no harm to any of it.

(So what happened? What did *Christ*ianity do after the only real Christian died on the cross? It killed millions of human beings because they were "evil." It ran swords and lances through the bodies of infidels and thought it was doing *good*. It went across the ocean and destroyed the Aztecs, Mayas, and Incas because they didn't *believe* in Jesus Christ. But Jesus Christ would never have killed a living creature, unless perhaps that creature was trying to kill him and other innocent peace-loving people. But he surely would never have killed one single solitary Inca, Aztec, Maya, and other American "Indian" because that person didn't believe in *Him*. He didn't believe in *Him*, not the man that Paul claimed was the son of Jehovah who had been crucified on the cross to save men from their sins so they could all meet in heaven. No, he didn't believe in any of that. He believed in this life. He knew nothing of another life. He was too honest for that… God eventually lived over 2,000 years. He travelled around the world and saw with his own eyes what the "Christians" did to each other and non-Christians. Eventually he killed himself.)

SEVEN

Mary still kept a garden behind the small one-room house. Poor people stole from it sometimes, but she considered she was giving rather than they taking. There were figs and dates, beans and cucumbers, and a small patch of coriander. From the day God was able to walk, Mary would take him to the garden with her so he would learn to appreciate what comes from the earth. After some years one conversation went thus:

Mother Mary, where do you think this all comes from?

I don't know dear God, but I love it. Is there anything better than a fresh fig?

Do you think figs – and all plants – exist for "a reason?"

What do you mean?

The Jews say Jehovah put plants and animals on the

earth for us… Do you think everything exists for "us?"

I have absolutely no idea God. No one knows. People always talk about "reasons" for things existing… and the "reasons" are usually related to themselves. People love to put themselves at the center of the universe. But it is very possible that nothing – absolutely nothing – exists "for a reason." It might be that all existence "just exists" and people are part of it like plants, animals, rocks, rivers, clouds, rain, and the sun.

Do you mean that we are no more important than a fig or a cucumber?

I didn't say that. This is something your father and I often talked about. Just because there is no "guiding hand" behind life doesn't mean that life is not important. Every creature must decide for itself what is important.

When you think of the world that way everything changes…

Of course it does. The rabbis no longer tell you what is important. Nor do the Romans or anyone else. You, God, must decide for yourself, and I, Mary, must decide for myself. This is one of the "reasons" why your father saw the world so differently from other people. He didn't put man and Jehovah on top of the hierarchy of "life". He saw no hierarchy. He saw a great struggle for power. The Jews with their Jehovah, the Romans with their deities and laws and armies, animals eating plants, men eating animals, the Romans conquering the Jews, and on and on. Your father used to say that if cucumbers had teeth, they would eat animals and maybe even us. None of this means that one thing is necessarily "better" or "worse" than another. The question is really what controls what.

So Mother, where should I look to know what is good or bad, right or wrong?

There is only one place to look and that is into your own heart.

How will I know how I should live?

Will you "know" or "feel"…? Your head and your heart will talk to each other, play with each other, and even sometimes fight with each other.

And who will win – my head or my heart?

That is for you to discover my dear God. But actually in the end they might be inextricably linked together. They might always decide everything together. That is part of the great mystery.

But Mother, everyone talks about there being good and evil in the world. Don't laws and commandments tell us the difference?

Dear God, all laws and commandments are made by people. The Romans have their version of good and bad. Pontius Pilate has his good and bad. The Jews have their good and bad. The man who beats his donkey thinks he is doing good, but maybe he is doing bad. Of course most people justify their good and bad with deities, a Jehovah, and so-called prophets. Your father believed in none of them. He was his own god, his own prophet. But he used to say that most people's ideas of good and bad were built into their systems like the blood that flows through their veins. He did not think most people were strong enough to create their own vision of good and evil.

I wish Father were here to talk with us.

So do I God. I do my best to tell you what he thought.

I'm getting hungry. Can we eat a cucumber and some figs?

But first we'll ask them if they want to be eaten.

But they can't talk…

If they could, what do you think they would say?
God and Mary both laughed and went inside to prepare some food.

EIGHT

One day God was alone in the house. Sunlight was flowing in through the open door. He sensed something move in the corner of the room near the table where he and his mother ate. He approached it and saw that it was a baby lizard. The animal scurried against the wall and frantically began to climb. It fell back and tried to hide in a corner. God would never harm a lizard or any small animal, but the lizard did not know this. It appeared petrified with fear. God wanted to pick it up so that he could put it outside and set it free. What would happen outside? Would it get eaten by a bird or a larger animal? What would it kill to eat and survive? God was not able to catch it with his fingers. It slipped away every time. Finally he began to "guide" it toward the door. With his cupped hands he was able to alter its direction as it moved about frenetically. God was relieved when it finally ran out the door. "Have I done something good?" he wondered. "How long will the lizard survive outside *in the world?* Maybe I should have tried to keep it in the house. Maybe I should have protected it…"

God was perplexed. How did one know what one should do?

NINE

After the lizard had left the room, God went to work on a pair of shoes for a Roman soldier. While he worked his mind was still on the question that was so central to him: *How should one live?* When he looked around at the world, it seemed that most people did not think excessively about this question. People rarely talked deeply about the moral quandary, the quagmire of "right" and wrong." Most people just lived. Donkeys didn't ask themselves how they should live – whether or not they should bay loudly or softly, walk fast or slowly, kick someone in the leg or butt. No, they just lived. It seemed most Jews and Romans were the same: the Jews did what Jews do and the Romans did what Romans do. They didn't ask many questions. If they did, they seemed satisfied with simple or paltry

28

answers. They didn't search their souls. If they did, their souls were not very fertile gardens. — But some people were much more agreeable than others. Had they *decided* to be nice? Or was it just their characters? Was it just the way they were? And the people who were unkind or unpleasant? Had they searched their hearts and *decided* to be that way? How much *decision-making* actually went into the way people were?

God thought and God wondered.

He finished the shoes, drank some wine, and lay down on his bed. The sun was low, but Mary was still at the marketplace. His mind continued to wander. He couldn't put chains on it and keep it from wandering. It ran where it wanted to run. His mind was not a prison. Perhaps it was a prisoner run free...

The lizard: Where did it come from? Did it have a purpose in life? How long would it live? Would any other lizard or creature care when it died? Would I have made its life better had I kept it in the house? How long before it gets eaten by another animal? Why is this world so cruel? Why should I care about a lizard? — The man Paul keeps telling me that my father was the son of Jehovah and that he has been resurrected from the dead and is now in heaven. I have seen nothing dead come back to life. Why would Jehovah suddenly choose my father to be the first to come back to life? What about all the people who died before him? Didn't Jehovah care about them? — My mother tells me that

Jesus would often look at the sky and shudder. His whole body would tingle as he felt the mystery... the mystery of it all... All... ALL. She says the only thing that held him to the earth was their love. I am beginning to be like my father. I am in a constant state of wonderment. When I walk outside and look at people and what they do and how they spend their time on this earth, I think, 'They are so similar to animals, herd animals, except whereas birds fly and lizards crawl, they walk on two feet'. I am one of them. Do this, do that. Follow this, follow that... Why? Why? What should I, God Magdalene Christ, follow? Who should I follow? How should I spend the time that I have from now until my death? Is there a "good" way to live? How does one know when one is being "good?" And good to whom? Should others count more than myself? Should people count more than animals? Should the Jews count more than the Romans? Should I let Paul tell lies about my father? Should I try to stop him? Should I shut him up forever? Should I just shut my mouth and follow the laws of the Jews when I am with the Jews and the Romans when they wield the power? Or should I, God, create my own laws? Should I be a law unto myself? Should I want followers like Paul does? Mother says that Jesus followed nobody and wanted no followers. Should I try to prevent Paul from making a religion based on my father? Maybe a religion based on my father would be better than what the Jews or Romans have to offer...

But Paul and his friends are distorting my father! They are turning what he said inside out! They are crucifying him a second time!

Just then God heard Mary's footsteps outside the door. When she entered the house there was enough light such that he could see that she was crying.

TEN

But in a sense, they were tears of joy.

Why are you crying, Mother? God's long body was spread across the blanket on his bed. Mary came and sat beside him.

I was thinking about your father.

So was I… What were you thinking about?

The day he died… According to the Julian calendar, it was exactly seventeen years ago.

God said nothing.

I think I have told you that I was the last person there, at the foot of the cross. Paul and the others had left hours before when Jesus stopped talking. I slept curled in this blanket against the wooden plank with you in my belly. It was the longest night of my life. In a sense, you saved me God. The last drops of blood of the man I loved were dripping from above me. You were inside me. Our baby. The creation of a dead man and a living woman. I hated the world. I wanted to follow Jesus to the grave. I wanted to ask a Roman soldier to run his sword through my gut. But you were there. I hated the world outside of me, but I loved what was inside of me.

O Mother…

You cannot imagine the emotion I felt that night. All of me wanted to die and all of me wanted to live. To die with the man I loved… To live with the baby inside of me…

God whispered, *How can the world be so cruel?*

Mary answered, *How can the world provide so much love? I felt both emotions at the same time. Can you imagine, dear God, all the beauty and all the ugliness at the same moment? You cannot know how I felt until you love someone like I loved your father…*

Maybe it will never happen. Maybe I will never find such love.

My greatest prayer is that you do.

But you never pray, Mother…

Life is a prayer… every day… every moment…

A prayer to whom?

To oneself and those one loves and cares about.

But didn't my father care about all life?

Yes, he did. And his prayer was always for every living creature. But he knew it was hopeless. He knew there was no one to answer his prayer. In the end, he said love was the only divinity.

Is that what he talked about before he died?

Really God, he talked about what he always talked about… loving the world, this world, the only world we have… He talked about the great unfathomable mystery of this world… He talked about the innocence of all creation… He said even his killers were innocent in that they could not help being the fools that they were… But more than anything else, he talked about how much he loved me and how lucky we were to have met. Without each other, we never would have known what love is.

And I would never have known what life is…

They were both talking through tears.

God, my darling son, in the end, what is "life?" Isn't "life" different for everyone. Doesn't every creature live living in its own unique way… This is why love is so rare. This is why your father and I loved each other so much… Because he was the one person on earth who made me feel that I was not alone. He and I had similar eyes, ears, and thoughts. Our bodies and minds never felt separate. And O how I loved him and how he loved me. Sometimes it was almost as if when I loved him I was loving myself, and in loving myself I was loving the world, and loving the world always brought me back to loving him. It was a huge cycle… one that neither of us could stop.

You saved each other…

Yes, you could say that. God, the world gives you every reason to go crazy all the time. Every day. Every night. But love gives a reason to stay sane. First I had Jesus to love, now I have you. Now you have me and one day you will find the woman with whom the world can be made beautiful.

And if I don't…

Then you will be the opposite of me: I had no love with a mother, but I had love with a man; you will have had love with a mother, but never with a woman…

O mother…

The room was silent for a period of time that no one measured. God's eyes closed just as Mary kissed him on the forehead.

ELEVEN

God began to wander more and work less. The money he brought in for his shoes was not essential to their survival. There was enough food in the garden for them to eat and Mary sold the excess at the marketplace. He would usually work for a few hours in the morning, then prepare a sack with a little food and drink, and set off for the hills and orchards. Sometimes he would meet Joshua, but most of the time he walked alone. There was an old man who tended sheep outside of Nazareth with whom he had become friends. He didn't know the man's name nor did the man know his. But it didn't matter. Why would it matter? Sometimes the sun went halfway across the sky while they walked and talked.

For a few days Mary didn't feel well and stayed in bed. God nursed her and went himself to the marketplace to sell the vegetables. When she was better, God went back to wandering in the afternoons. He met the old man…

Ah, there you are. I haven't seen you for a while.

No, my mother was a bit ill and I had to take the vegetables to the marketplace. But she is better now.

What was it?

I don't know. She was tired and said her blood felt heavy.

Blood is one of the strangest things on earth. Not really, actually. It's no stranger than bones or skin or teeth or the moon when it gets cut in half.

Where does blood come from?

Where does water come from? Where does your tongue come from? Where do these sheep come from…? When I kill a sheep and watch the blood pour from its body, I always think that men and sheep have much in common. Life can be taken away so easily. We both have blood that the blade of a knife can drain from our bodies and in a matter of minutes we are dead.

When you kill a sheep, do you look inside at the rest of the body? What is in there? Are there parts that serve no purpose, or does everything seem to do something to keep us alive?

I don't know. But the insides of a man and the insides of a sheep are not that different.

You have seen dead men cut open?

A few times.

And are their insides similar to those of a sheep? Is one more complicated than the other?

That is hard to say. Is the moon more complicated than the sun? Is a fig more complicated than a rock? Is a serpent more complicated than Herod? How can one judge? How can one know what things are really made of?

Isn't the life of a man more complicated than that of a fig or a sheep?

I don't know. Sometimes I think it is useless to talk about things being simple or complicated. If everything is part of the same universe, then perhaps everything shares certain qualities of "existence." Then other times I think everything is different… that every existing thing is a universe unto itself and that there is no real way to compare different parts. I don't know.

Does anyone know?

Many pretend to…

There was a moment of silence and then God said,

Do you know you have become kind of a father to me? I never knew my father as he died before I was born.

Better your father than your mother, the shepherd chuckled… *She would have taken you with her into the world of the dead. Do you know who your father was?*

Yes, that I do. His name was Jesus… Jesus of Nazareth. Maybe you have heard of him. Some people still talk about him even though he has been dead for seventeen years.

No, I don't know him. I rarely go to the marketplace. Other than you, my friend, I talk exclusively with my sheep. How did your father die?

Nailed to a cross like many common criminals. Pontius Pilate sentenced him to death for disturbing the peace in the land.

What did he do? Was he a violent man?

Absolutely not. He was as gentle as your lambs. At least that is what my mother says.

Then how did he disturb the peace?

Some people spread the rumor that he claimed to be the son of Jehovah and that people should follow him instead of the Romans and Jews.

And did he make such a claim?

No, to the contrary. My mother says he did not even believe in the Jewish god Jehovah. He did not believe in any gods… not the Roman gods, the Greek gods, or the Jewish god. He saw no proof of any divinity. He did not have an explanation for where the world came from. He thought it was all a great mystery.

He could have been my friend. The more I stare at the hills and sky, the more I am filled with wonder. What I have learned is that men are just like sheep… They have to follow somebody. They need a master. There are few masters and many sheep.

My father wanted no followers. He wanted people to think for themselves. He asked many questions and gave few answers. But then a man named Paul started saying that he was the son of Jehovah and that when he spoke, he spoke the word of Almighty God.

The Romans and the Jews certainly must not have liked that.

They didn't. He was judged a troublemaker and the Romans crucified him. And then, after he died, this man Paul claimed he was "resurrected", had gone to his Father in heaven, and that he had died for the sins of mankind. Can you imagine that? My father never talked about "sin" in his life. He never talked about Jehovah. He never talked about heaven. The only thing he talked about was respecting life and loving the world and each other. According to my mother, he loved her with every drop of blood in his body. And she loved him equally.

They were lucky to have had love. It is so rare. And you were lucky to be the fruit of the tree of their love. Most of us are the fruit of another kind of tree, a tree of random haphazard coupling.

Sometimes I think everything is random and haphazard.

I like to think not. But maybe it is so. Whenever I must choose a sheep to kill my mind says, "Why should this one die and not that one?" And there is no answer.

Do you think life is as precious to sheep as it is to men?

I don't know. I don't know what goes on in the mind of a sheep. But I do know that most men do not act as if life is precious at all. They treat it with so little respect.

They kill animals and each other without a thought.

I think that was really my father's message: love life and respect life.

But what is this thing called "life?" Each man has his own definition…

And maybe each sheep does too.

You have an interesting mind, my friend… So tell me, what do you do in this life to have money to eat?

I make shoes. I usually work in the morning then walk in the afternoon.

The old man looked at God's feet. *Can you make me a pair of shoes like those you are wearing? I have a little money. I can pay you. They will be my last shoes before I die.*

One never knows when death will come, except when one is nailed to a cross.

It is such a barbaric practice. For some things the Romans are civilized. For others they are ugly beasts.

God and the old man's eyes met, then God looked at the sky.

The sun is getting low. I must be going.

Yes, and come back soon.

I will. With your shoes.

God knelt down on the ground and opened his hand wide to measure the length of the old man's feet.

I will start on them tomorrow.

Thank you, my friend.

Goodbye. Till we meet again.

Yes, till we meet again.

TWELVE

Mary noticed that her son was not as happy as he used to be. As a child the world had been God's playground. All things were to be enjoyed. The earth and his mind were weightless. Now Mary sensed that God, like his father before him, needed to be careful lest he go crazy. She too had almost gone crazy. The problem – the equation – is really not that complicated:

If you truly care about creatures (human beings included) other than yourself, if you truly try to put yourself in other creatures' shoes even knowing all the while that this is impossible, if you understand that every creature is the center of its own universe, if you give "value" to all other creatures knowing all the while that there is no "equality" among them, if when you see a dead creature your body cringes because you see and feel that a whole universe has died (each creature being a universe unto itself), if you believe large and small mean nothing when it comes to the value of a creature, if when you see a dead creature you imagine the tragedy and suffering before death, if when you share in the suffering you are not just thinking about your own condition of suffering and feeling sorry for yourself (like people often do when they cry at funerals, not because they are sad for the person in the coffin and that person's surviving loved ones, but because they are thinking about their own eventual death), if you think the world never has been and never will be a "fair" and "just" place, if you do not believe there is some divine hand that is guiding the universe and will eventually "take care of things" and make sure some kind of heavenly justice is served, if you think all things are simply "there" (neither divine nor superfluous), if you doubt that your eyes see "reality", if you think every moment and every "thing" is infinitely complex, if you do not believe in a creator or a creation because you think that such an idea just begs a question, if you think the human mind might very well be incapable of knowing truth, if you think the idea of truth is more than likely a human invention that has nothing to do with the world, if you think that Being simply is and always has been and always will be, if you think that nothing can be other than what it is, if you think there is no such thing as freedom of the will, if you understand that every second there is tragedy and suffering and death somewhere, if when you look at the sky you understand that there is no up or down in the universe, if you sense that the earth is a tiny speck in what is probably finitely infinite space… then insanity is a real possibility.

But so is love…

Mary knew this. She knew that someone as sensitive and thinking as God could easily go off the deep end. She knew that love had kept her and Jesus from going crazy. Their love for each other had allowed them to stay afloat on the vast sea of wonder, horror, pain, joy, beauty, solitude, ugliness, uncertainty, suffering, ecstasy, and mystery that is existence. The chariot of their love carried them across all the mountains, deserts, valleys, oceans, pits, and fires of the world until Jesus was nailed to the cross. When the Roman soldiers came the next morning and Mary watched them take down the cross and detach the body of the man she loved, she did not go crazy because she had God in her belly. Now it was her turn to help God.

THIRTEEN

For a moment, let us imagine that God did not live around the time of Jesus, but rather at the beginning of the 21st century. Let us imagine he was born in some corner of Western Civilization (even Nazareth today could probably fit our purposes.) God would most certainly have a television, an iPhone, an iPad, and a computer and would spend close to half his day in front of a screen. He would constantly be bombarded by text messages, tweets, emails, phone calls, and millions of images and words. There would also be school to worry about, a huge variety of music to listen to (though "pop" and "hip-hop" would probably have the upper hand,) decisions to make about what clothes to wear, what to put in one's body, and what other bodies to spend time with. God then and God today would likely be two very different Gods. Or would they? Would one God be kinder? Would one God be more reflective? Would one God be his own man? (Is it possible to be your own man at any stage in "history?") Would one God be closer to other men? Would one God ask more questions? Would one have fewer answers? Would one be more capable of love? — Normally we think of God as being outside of time and space, outside of "culture", outside "the world", outside of a context, outside of "history." But is this fair to God? Is it fair to any part of the universe to think that it is somehow not part of the universe? Is it possible for even a thinking God to have one thought that is not somehow conditioned by the world? Is it possible for a mind to think outside the world if that mind is part of the world? — Maybe this is where the idea of "a soul" came from – from a human craving and longing to get away from the world – *"O please dear Lord, free me from the suffering and toil of this life!…There must be more than this body and this decaying flesh!…There must be more to my humanness!…There must be a "spirit", a "soul" that is outside the rubble of this earth!…There has to be something better than this…body!"* But our God has a body and he lives in time and space. Whether he is the son of Jesus and Mary in Nazareth or the son of Mr. and Mrs. James P. Coleman in New York City, in either case he has a so-called *body* and a so-called *mind* that must carry him through "life." And God wonders what makes his body move and what makes his mind decide. What pushes him to say this or that, to go here or there, to listen to this or that music, wear these or those clothes, to accept or to question, to love or to hate, to follow or to lead? Is he "free?" Is any piece of the universe – human, godly or otherwise – actually *free* to think or do anything separate from "the universe?" Is not every piece of the universe *built* into the universe? Surely nature is not separate and free, so why would God be? — God is trying to be free. This is why we have named him God. He is trying to make sense of the whole bag of beans in his own way. He is trying to live his own life and not a life imposed on him by the world. But he has the intelligence, honesty, and courage to wonder if it is possible. He knows that most men and animals are prisoners of their bodies and minds and the culture that surrounds them. He knows it is very possible that all being is a prisoner of Being and that there is no god or moral imperatives, and that living and dying are not part of any "plan." And he knows that if such is the case, he has no choice but to make his own way. He must become God. Now. Before it is too late.

FOURTEEN

A few days after his last talk with the old man, his mother wasn't feeling well again.

I don't think I can go to the market today, God.

It's okay, I can go. I will quickly finish a pair of shoes I am making for the old man, and then I will go sell the vegetables.

They can wait until tomorrow.

No, I'll go. Then in the afternoon I will take the shoes to the old man.

I'm just feeling tired. My body only wants to sleep.

What do you think is wrong, Mother?

Maybe I am just getting old.

You are not old.

Either I'm getting old for the world or the world is getting old for me. Death should come when one is tired of the world.

Mother, I will make a fire and give you some tea. That will help.

Thank you, my son.

God made the tea, finished the shoes, and went to the market wondering what life would be like without his mother. He had never truly imagined the thought before. He had never "felt" the idea that one day Mary would no longer be there when he came home. She was like his bed. It would always be there. As long as their little house was there, his bed would be there… and his mother would be there! But no! O God! Mothers die! Beds don't die! Mothers die! All mothers die!

God's spine went cold at the thought.

FIFTEEN

Joshua found God at the marketplace.

I went to your house expecting to find you, but I found your mother. She doesn't look well, God.

She's tired. Her life has not been easy. But then again, whose life is easy?

That is a very good question. I think life is easiest for people who forget they are alive. They are so busy with their lives that they never wonder about anything, never question anything, never doubt anything, and never really think about anything. Marcus tells me that is the way a lot of soldiers are. They just kill or get killed. They never ask why they are fighting, why they are killing, or why someone is trying to kill them. They are machines, not men.

Aren't most men machines, Joshua?

Probably. Look at the Jews. They all think the same.

It makes life simple.

Do you talk to Marcus often? Have you decided he is your father?

We have both decided he is my father.

That's good.

But God, I want to talk to you about your father. This man Paul is really using him. And people are starting to believe him. Even some Jews are listening to his nonsense.

Yes, I know. What have you heard him saying?

He is promising eternal life in heaven for everyone who is baptized in the river and who follows him and his friends John, Luke, and Matthew. He is calling himself a "Christian" and saying that Jesus Christ was the son of Jehovah and came on earth to save the world.

What he says has nothing to do with what my father, Jesus Christ, said and believed. Paul is just another lost soul trying to find a place for himself, trying to be important, and trying to turn life into something that it is not. Were my father alive he would laugh at such babble… Actually he wouldn't laugh, he probably would have felt empathy for his friend Paul… another weak man who needs crutches to walk through life.

But he is not alive to defend himself. He is not alive to tell people that what Paul is saying is a pile of lies.

Maybe the Romans will kill Paul for disturbing the peace.

I think even some of the Romans are starting to

listen to him.

What an absurd irony. First they kill my father and then they worship him!

I hear some Romans saying they have too many gods. It is easier to have just one.

People will believe anything. The longer I live the crazier the world looks.

For me too.

Are you hungry? Here, have some figs. I will never sell them all today. I brought too many. And besides, I must take a pair of shoes to an old man outside of town. He's a shepherd… In fact, why don't you come with me. He's an interesting man. He has become kind of like my father…

Now we both have fathers…

They laughed and together went to see the old man and his sheep.

SIXTEEN

I see you have a friend with you today.

He's really my only friend, except for you and my mother.

Your friend will be my friend. How is your mother?

She's not feeling so well again. I went to the market in her place this morning. But I finished your shoes first. Here they are.

How wonderful. I have not had shoes for years. My feet have been my shoes, like the feet of my sheep. Let me try them and see if they fit on the beaten feet of an old man… Ah, yes… Thank you so much.

It is my pleasure to make shoes for friends.

I have some coins to give you. They have been with me for weeks, since I killed and sold the meat of one of my animals.

The old man pulled money from a pocket.

I do not need nor want your denarii.

Then give them to your friend or your mother.

Give them to your sheep.

What can my sheep do with money?

They can buy shoes…

The old man laughed, then he took a few steps in his new shoes.

It's odd to have something between my feet and the ground. With shoes, one doesn't know what one is stepping on.

Animals always do.

But they don't see what they step on in the same way we do. They don't differentiate between "rocks", "dirt", "mud", and "grass", like we do. They live in a different world. I'm not sure which world, but I'm sure their world is very different from yours and mine. What fascinates me is how they will follow me wherever I go. For years… for their whole lives they will follow me.

That is not so different from people. Look at the Jews following their rabbis and the Romans following their leaders.

You are right. There is little difference.

I wonder how big the world is and how many different things there are that people follow. All we know are the Jews and the Romans, but maybe there are other peoples with other ideas all over the world. Maybe there are even "free" people who have no rabbis or Roman generals to follow.

I doubt it, but who knows?

What is the world, anyway? We talk about it, but no one knows what it is. We walk on it, but we don't know what is under the ground. No one has been to the end of the world. No one knows if it has an end. Maybe it goes on forever.

I have spent my life here with sheep. My father had sheep. His father had sheep. Beyond that I know nothing.

And I have spent my life around Nazareth. The farthest I have been is maybe walking three hours. Then I came back home. The Romans have come from Rome. But where is that? I have no idea. You have no idea. How can anyone who has never been there have any idea?

What amazes me is how little we know about anything, yet people are satisfied with the paltry answers they have. We have absolutely no idea about where the world came from, how it works, where it is going, how man and animals and everything else got here, how our minds and bodies function, what is in our blood, how we breathe and think and decide… yet everybody acts like they are "at home" in the world, like they have their "place" in the world, like the world makes sense. But "sense?" What is "sense?" It is the same for sheep. Look at them… They feel like the whole universe is in its proper place.

As long as they have grass to chew on and water to drink.

Yes. Look at what men need. Food, wine, a bed,

someone to follow, companionship…

We are simple creatures.

But some of us are simpler than others. Some are more complicated. Some are not satisfied with the answers…

Just like some sheep that bay louder than others. Some even try to run away from the herd.

Yes, it is the same with men.

I don't think I can ever be satisfied with what a rabbi or Roman tells me about anything.

Nor a Greek…

Nor anyone… even myself. My mind will never be satisfied. Even with itself.

Do you think a mind can fuse with another mind?

It is rare, but I see no reason why it can't happen. You said your mother and father had fused before he was killed on the cross.

Yes, that is what my mother told me.

So why would fusing with another person be desirable? That is a question I cannot answer because it has never happened to me. If I have fused with anything it is with my sheep.

My mother says one doesn't know what it is until it happens. It is what the world calls "love".

But maybe it is not a "thing," maybe it is never the same from two lovers to the next, maybe every love is as different as the sun and the moon.

We don't even know what the sun and moon are.

No, we don't.

We know so little about anything.

You know, I have been tending sheep my whole life. Compared to most lives it has been long. I am old. Most people can never say that. I have had more time to think than the majority of people who visit the earth.

Why do you say, "visit the earth?"

Isn't that what it is? A visit is when you go some place and don't stay. That is what we all do in this world. Perhaps if you think of life as a visit, you will feel it differently… So let me tell you about one of my favorite thoughts. I say "favorite" because it is one that comes to me often. It is a thought that makes me want to laugh and cry at the same time.

Aren't those the best kind of thoughts?

Certainly.

So tell us your thought…

It is this: I will use myself as the example. Oneself is what one should know best, but that might not be true at all. But it doesn't matter in this case — in the case of my thought… So here it is: I ask myself, "What is your origin? Where do you come from? How did you get here? How did you come to be?" Now of course you can ask the same questions for absolutely everything that exists, but for now we will only ask it for me.

It is a very good question.

So let us look at the answer… Maybe I should say let us look for the answer because it is possible we won't find an answer to look at… But let us look. For me to be in this world, my mother and father had to have been in this world and had to have come together to make me. They are the only two people I ever saw that have to do with my existing. I never saw their parents who had to exist for me to exist. They were long dead before I was born. But think… their parents had their own parents and their parents' parents had their own parents, and on and on and on… But back to when? That is the question nobody asks or thinks about. Back to when? For every single person who is in the ancestral line of my existence, there had to have been two parents to make him or her… No one just "appeared" out of nowhere. At least, I don't think they did.

I don't either…

So…so…do you see what I am saying…or thinking? My existence goes back forever and ever. It makes no sense to think I had "a beginning". And now is when I laugh… Everything else that exists is the same. Nothing – absolutely nothing – "had a beginning!" Everything goes back forever! You, your friend, those sheep, the sun, the moon, the pebbles under my new shoes… Everything! And now I cry! What does this mean? It means there is no origin of anything! We can never know the origin of anything because there is no origin to anything because everything goes back forever and ever and ever! Everything… forever! This is the thought of the old man with the sheep…

I wonder if anyone else has ever had this thought?

I don't know. It doesn't matter. If they have, then I

have a friend.

It is a beautiful thought.

I am just glad to have been able to tell it to someone. I have had it for a long time, but I have had no one to share it with because everyone else will just start telling me about Jehovah or the Roman or Greek gods that supposedly "created everything!" The same old tired answers are immediately always given. But my thought is not old and tired. It is lovely and frightening at the same time.

It is almost not "human"…

Actually when I have it, it makes me dizzy.

But sometimes it is good to be dizzy.

As long as you can settle back to the earth… O the earth! O what a place! What a wonder!

There was a silence even among the sheep. God, Joshua, and the old man could all hear themselves breathing. Finally God said he should to be going to see how his mother was feeling.

Come back soon. It is nice to have some company.

We will.

And maybe it's time you started looking for a little of that love we talked about.

Can one look for it?

I don't know. I've never known what it is.

Maybe it is not too late.

I'm as old as your grandfathers.

The ones I never knew. The only person tied to me that I have known is my mother. But in a sense, you

are the father I never knew.
And you are the son I never had.
Now you have two…
We are as silly as the sheep.
Sillier perhaps.
They need me. I need thee.
Every hour…
Thank you for the shoes.
Thank you for the thoughts.
Till we meet again…
Yes, till we meet again…

SEVENTEEN

Spring passed, the days lingered, the olives grew, the donkeys bayed in the morning but were quiet at the end of the day as the heat sapped their energy. There was relative peace in the area of Palestine. As long as they obeyed the laws, the Romans basically left the Jews alone to live and worship as they pleased. God and Mary resided on the edge of the Jewish part of town, but of course they were considered "bad" Jews because they were never seen at the synagogue. Their minds had been corrupted by "the devil", the devil being the force behind all things "un-Jewish". But God and Mary were nice to people and because of this were somewhat of an enigma. How can you not worship Jehovah and still be a good person? But not only were God and Mary good to others, they did not try to force their "disbeliefs" or doubts on others. They let the Jews be Jews and respected them in their beliefs and practices. They just did not share their view of the world for a thousand reasons.

One thing, however, was certain: No Jewish parents wanted their daughter to consider marrying a man like God. *No… no… and no!* A Jewish girl was not to marry a man who did not follow the laws of the Torah!

But children do not always do what their parents want. Even two thousand years ago – eighteen years after the death of Jesus Christ – there were boys and girls going against the will of their parents. God, of course, was not one of them as his relationship with his mother was such that he had nothing to rebel against. They loved and respected each other and they shared the same doubts about what was considered "truth." God questioned all the values and beliefs of the world around him. That was enough…

Naomi, however, was a very different story. By the time she had her first menstrual period she was at war with her parents, particularly her father. Initially it had not been an open war. It had been silent and private. She was the third offspring in a devoutly Jewish family of five children. For years she kept her ideas to herself. When the family repeated the same prayers before every meal, she thought it was ridiculous. Was Jehovah deaf? Couldn't He remember they had prayed a few hours before? Why did they have to say the same things a thousand times? When a lamb was sacrificed on the day of the Passover, she thought it was barbaric. Why would God want innocent animals killed in His name? She watched her parents choose a man to marry for her older sister. Her sister didn't love the man and Naomi thought the man had no more character than a rag with which one dries one's face. He never thought for himself. He only followed traditions. How could her sister spend her life with such a boring man?

When it was Naomi's turn to have a husband, the war became open. Naomi could stay silent no more. She wanted her own man or no man. She could not let her father choose a husband for her. That was impossible! Her body told her it was impossible. Her mind told her it was impossible. Her whole being told her it was impossible. *Where is it written in this universe,* she thought, *that a girl should be required to spend her life on earth with a man she doesn't love, especially a man that she has not chosen herself?*

When she was sixteen Naomi saw two possibilities: she could run away or she could go crazy. But where could she run to? She knew that girls alone in the world quickly became slaves or victims of cruel unsavory men. She knew that if she ran away she would likely be shortening her life. But what life? She couldn't live "the life" that her parents had planned for her. She looked at her body: *I cannot share this with a man I don't love. She looked into her mind: I cannot spend my life with a man that I cannot talk to and with whom I have nothing in common.* She thought of killing herself. Other girls had done so.

But fortunately, before she ran too far away or killed herself, she met God, not the invisible God of many so-called "holy" books, but God the man with flesh and blood, the beloved son of Mary Magdalene and Jesus Christ.

Miraculously or not, God saved Naomi and Naomi saved God.

EIGHTEEN

Their meeting was like all meetings. The infinite circumstances of their lives had led them to be in the same place at the same time. This happens every day to essentially everyone. You go somewhere and there are other human beings. You meet some. But what doesn't happen every day is that you fall in love with one of them. No one calls it "fate" when you don't fall in love. No one talks about "destiny" or things being "meant to be" with regard to the thousands of people you meet that you don't care about in any special way. But when you do meet someone and fall in love, many people want to call it the work of "fate", "destiny", "god", "gods", "cosmic design", or some other such term. Or, on the other side of the intellectual fence, there are those who want to say that such happenings – even *all* happenings – are "random", "chance", the "luck of the dice"… But what if neither is the case? What if neither "destiny" nor "chance" has anything to do with the world? What if these are just human terms to try to "explain things" to the insecure human head? What if everything just "is?" What if there is no god or purpose behind anything? And what if there is no random chaos either? What if all being – the entire universe, the totality of all existence – just "exists?" Then what do we call the meeting of God and Naomi…?

Naomi had run away. Not far, not forever. Just away. The night before, her father had told her that the Holy Spirit had destined her to marry Isaac. She responded that Isaac meant less to her than the family donkey. She wouldn't do it. She would die first. Her father ordered her to get down on her knees, pray to Jehovah, and repent her multitude of sins. She refused. He screamed at her. She was a "sinner!" She was "evil!" The devil had taken her! She would "rot in hell!" Her head and body were on fire. She ran for the door and her father was not able to catch her. She fled to the olive orchard on the hill where she spent the night. Fortunately, it was summer.

Mary was feeling a little better, but God had helped her take the vegetables to the marketplace in the early morning. When the stand was ready for business, he left his mother and went for a long walk and thought about everything and nothing. On the hill in the orchard sitting next to a tree was a girl. She seemed to be sobbing. God wasn't sure of that until he got closer.

Hello…

She did not look at him.

Hello…

The eyes furtively glanced his way, then she buried her face in her hands. God knelt down next to her and spoke softly.

I do not think I know you. Have we ever met before?

The girl said nothing, but sensed that the voice certainly meant no harm.

May I sit here for a moment? If I am bothering you, if you want me to go away, I will leave like the stars in the morning.

Minutes passed. Neither said anything. The sobs became less frequent. Finally it was the girl who spoke.

I saw lots of stars this night. I didn't know there were so many stars.

You slept here?

I didn't sleep much, but I was here.

Do you have no home?

I have a home where I no longer want to go.

Why is that?

There is nothing for me there.

Are your parents dead?

No, I am dead.

God tried to imagine what she meant. He looked at the girl's bare feet.

I am a shoemaker. If you have no shoes, I could make you some.

I have shoes. I just didn't have them on when I ran out the door.

You ran away?

Yes.

Last night?

Yes.

Do you want to tell me what you ran away from?

From a father who insists that I marry a man for whom I have no love.

Love is rare inside and outside of marriage.

Not only do I have no love for this man, but, like I told my father, I have no more feeling for him than for a donkey.

Maybe it is easier to love a donkey than a man.

I wouldn't know. I have never loved either. We have no donkey and…

She didn't finish her sentence.

I imagine your father and your father's father and your father's father's father are all Jews. Your father wants you to marry a Jew. You must marry a Jew…

I wouldn't mind marrying a Jew if I could find one I loved.

Maybe if you got to know the man your father wants you to marry you would love him.

Who knows? Anyway, Jews don't care about love in marriage. They care about God. They are really married to their God... Jehovah. Their love for Him is all that counts.

And it's not that way for you?

How can I love God? I have no idea if He is real or not. I have prayed to Him a thousand times and never had an answer.

The same thing happened to me.

Are you Jewish?

Not really. My ancestors were, but I have no reason to believe that the Jews have more truth than the Romans.

Your parents don't force you to believe things?

No. My mother is like me.

My parents force everything on me. Not just marriage. They want me to believe everything they believe. They want me to see the world exactly the way they see it. But that is ridiculous. Are we supposed to be exactly like our parents? Why can't they accept that I am different?

Because they think they have the truth.

Then it is a bad truth. No good truth would force a daughter to marry a man she didn't love. For them I am a black sheep in a family of white swans.

A black sheep can be as beautiful as a white swan.

Not according to my parents. They think I am the devil...

Have you tried to talk to them?

Of course I have. But they won't listen. Their minds are closed doors that never let in any fresh air. They don't think. They just follow the rabbis.

Maybe it is better if one doesn't think. People who don't think are often happy in their simple worlds. Maybe it is best for them to stay there.

I don't care if they stay there, but they should not force me to stay there with them. They cannot imagine that I am not made like they are and that I want a different life.

What life do you want?

I don't know. How could I know? I've been locked in my parents' cage for sixteen years. I've seen nothing else. I just know I don't want their life… She looks at God's face… Tell me, do you believe in hell?

No, I don't. I cannot imagine Jehovah being that cruel. But maybe he is.

Do you think He would send someone to hell for not being a Jew?

I can't believe He would ever punish someone who thought deeply and followed the dictates of his own conscience.

Maybe Jehovah is not just. Maybe He is cruel. Maybe He is like my father.

It is a possibility. Anything is possible. For me, the world is a great mystery. The older I get, the greater the mystery.

They were both silent. Both were staring into the orchard. Finally their heads turned and their eyes met.

The son of Jesus and Mary smiled and spoke.

We have talked all this time and we don't know each other's name. What is yours?

Naomi. And you?

God.

God!... O my God!

Both laughed and Naomi's weary head fell into God's lap.

NINETEEN

Mary was sitting up in bed. God was at her side. He took her hand and rubbed it.

Mother, today I met a girl… a woman.

Where did you meet her?

In the olive orchard.

How old is she?

Sixteen.

I think this is the first time in your life that you have come home and said, "Mother, I met a girl…"

It is the first time in my life that I have felt like this.

Like what…? You don't have to tell me. I can see it in your eyes.

I was taking my walk and I found her crying, sobbing under a tree.

Why? Let me guess? She is being forced to marry…

How did you know?

It is the tragic tradition in Judea. Our world does not know how to accommodate the human heart. Women are slaves to the civilization.

Aren't men also?

Yes, but in a different way. Women are there to keep the species alive. Men are there to decide who has power over the species.

You were never forced to marry. You were lucky.

I was not forced to marry because I had no parents who wanted me to uphold a family tradition. I had no family and no tradition. I was not forced to marry a man, but men forced me to do other things many times. I was only trying to survive…

And you never had a baby with those other men?

That is the miracle of my life. Only with your father – the only man I ever loved – did I produce a baby. You, dear God, are the apple that fell from the tree of the greatest love on earth. For that you are the luckiest man and I am the luckiest woman. So who is this girl you met in the orchard?

Before I tell you, tell me how you are feeling. How was the day?

I sold all the vegetables quickly, then I came back home to bed. My body just feels tired all the time. It is as if my arms and legs are ten times their normal weight and I must drag them around wherever I go.

O Mother, I know you will get better…

No, you don't know that. The only thing you know is that one day life will be sucked out of my body…

Mother...

God, one day I will die...

Yes, but...

It will happen when it happens

But not now... not yet...

Isn't it better to die too early than too late?

God squeezed his mother's hand and then rubbed each of her fingers.

Now tell me about the girl. I see love in your eyes and I want to know about the spark that started the fire.

Her name is Naomi. She is very strong of mind, but her body is as delicate as any flower. She ran away from her home last night when her father became violently angry because – like you said – she refuses to marry a man she doesn't love. She does not believe in the Jewish version of life. She has no idea why we are on earth. But she doesn't want to be told how to live. She wants to live her own life.

That is very hard to do in this world. Few people do it. Few people even think about doing it. We are all constantly pressured to act in certain ways. If it isn't parents pressuring you to obey, it's the Romans. If it isn't the Romans, it's the rabbis. If it isn't the rabbis, it's the congregation. Who can truly live his or her own life with all the social pressures people have? Your father and I were very lucky. We were pretty much able to live on the outskirts of society. But remember, he ended up dead on a cross.

He died too early.

Maybe, but maybe not.

He didn't deserve to die.

One thing is sure — his early death left me loving him forever.

Who really killed him, Mother?

The world killed him, just like the world kills everybody else. The world listened to Paul who made false claims about Jesus. The world took the easy way out. It usually does.

Well, Naomi is not taking the easy way. She refuses to follow her parents. She refuses to follow the Torah. She says she will die before she marries a man she doesn't love. She will die before she is forced to have babies with a man she doesn't love.

Where has she gone now? Where did she go when you said goodbye. Maybe you should have brought her here.

Maybe I should have. But she said she would go home one more time and try to reason with her parents.

She is courageous to try, but rarely can you reason with people who believe they possess "eternal truth" — especially people who are worried about the fiery judgment of Jehovah and the wicked judgment of the other people in their group.

We will see. We are meeting again tomorrow at the same time.

I would be worried that she might not be able to

come. Her father might not allow her to leave the house. She ran away once. He might not let her run away again… What does she look like, God?

Like an angel dropped from heaven.

That doesn't help. I have never seen an angel.

I have only seen one.

O my son, I'm happy for you. Do you think she loves you?

Today she fell asleep in my lap. For an hour I caressed her hair, neck, and shoulders.

And her sleeping body caressed yours…

Yes. I felt something I have never felt before. Everything about her fit perfectly into my eyes, ears, hands, and mind. I think she felt the same thing.

If you love each other, you will know. If one side feels doubt, it is not love… But let me warn you God, love is also a kind of slavery. We are slaves to the love. When I met your father, I could do nothing else but love him. It was impossible for me "not" to love him. I was a slave to him and my love for him. But I was also his master. Because he loved me madly in return, he was my slave. I could not help but follow him and he could not help but follow me. This is the great irony of love: you are both slave and master at the same time. You are enslaved by the love, but you only feel free when you are together.

O Mother…

Dear God, in one way love the simplest thing on earth. Either it is there or it isn't. If it is there, you will feel you are truly living only when you are together. If you love someone, there is always a hole in the world when you are apart.

I feel that hole now wanting and waiting to see her tomorrow.

Yes. Love itself is simple, but the world makes it complicated. The world is not kind to love. It almost always has other plans. It is jealous of love. It is vengeful. People who don't have love don't like to see others who do have it. I don't think most people even know what love is. I surely didn't until I met Jesus.

I will tell you soon if I have it and know what it is.

I would love to live to see my son living to love…

With that Mary got out of bed and prepared a meal for God. She herself was able to eat very little.

TWENTY

Naomi was there long before their scheduled meeting time. She had escaped the house in the middle of the night after her father had beaten her. He had thrashed her with a tree branch: three lashes for running away… three lashes for refusing to pray. That was his idea of justice. She had been in the olive grove for five hours when she finally saw God approaching.

You're already here. I thought I was early.

I ran away during the night. I've been here for a long time. I don't know how long. My father beat me yesterday. I don't know why I went home. I should have known. As soon as I walked in the house he started screaming. He threw me to the floor, bared my back and hit me. At least now I am free. I will never go back.

There were no tears in her voice. There was only

resolution.

Did he hit you with his hand?

No, I think it was a branch of a tree. It felt like a whip. But it doesn't matter now. I am gone. He will never beat me again.

But what if he finds you? He will certainly come looking for you.

I must hide, that's for sure. I must hide until he stops looking. Either that or I must run away.

She showed him the welts on her back.

It is still bleeding a little. We must go to my house. My mother said you should have come home with me yesterday.

She was right. I should have.

You can hide there and my mother can treat your back. I'm sure she has something to put on it.

Thank you, dear God. Thank you. All I want to do is get as far away as possible from the man who calls himself my father. All he has taught me is how not to live. Nothing will change him, so I must change my life. I want my mind to fly away… far away… like a bird flying to another land… Maybe it's not possible… I don't know, but I must try.

I will help you if I can.

Today it is hard to think of my father as a human being. Last night he was an uncontrollable animal. He would listen to nothing I tried to say. It was hopeless for me to argue or resist… I just wanted him to finish so I could run away.

Which direction is your house from here?

She pointed in the direction opposite from the one God had come.

That's good. We will be a decent distance from your home.

It is not my home anymore.

Do you have a scarf or any other clothes?

No. I brought nothing. I just got to the door, opened it, and ran.

My mother can give you a few things. She is home now. She didn't go to the market. She hasn't been feeling well lately.

I'm sorry.

Let's go now. If your father is looking for you, it's better for you to be in my house than out here in the open.

Yes.

Mary heard the door rattle and quickly sat up in bed.

Hello Mother. I am here with Naomi.

Hello, welcome Naomi. God has told me about you.

There is not much to tell, except that I have had to run away from my home.

Mother, her father beat her last night. The wounds on her back are still bleeding a little. Have we anything to put on them?

Yes, I will get it.

Mary rose very slowly from the bed and went to the

cupboard on the other side of the room.

You must stay with us for a few days, Naomi. Do you think your father is looking for you?

Probably, but last night he told me I should rot in hell. Maybe he's hoping the devil will accommodate me.

Nazareth is not that big. If he can't find you in a day or two, he will think you have fled to another town or perhaps have been taken by a Roman soldier. I was an orphan. I know what it is to be alone out there in Judea. Here you are safe for now.

Thank you Mary.

Don't thank me. Thank God. He found you in the orchard yesterday.

We found each other, Mother.

Of course… Naomi, come and sit on the bed. Let me see your back.

Naomi lifted her frock and Mary applied her ointment.

So he beat you because you refuse to marry the man he has chosen for you? Is that it?

Yes, but it is more than that. I just couldn't live the way he wanted me to live. It wasn't only about marriage.

It is always more complicated than meets the eye… Naomi, your back will be better in a few days. It might be hard to sleep tonight. Did you sleep last night?

No. Or just a little in the olive orchard.

You must be exhausted. Have you eaten?

No, but…

God, lay some bread and olives on the table. And some wine. Naomi must eat and then have a little sleep. She will have my bed while she is here.

No, I wouldn't think of it.

There is no thinking to do. God will sleep with you in the large bed and I will sleep in God's bed.

You're too kind.

One is never too kind. But some people are too unhappy to accept kindness. I'm sure you are not one of these people, Naomi.

I don't think so.

Mary finished treating the girl's back. They sat at the table together and God and Naomi ate. Mary tired quickly and was soon resting on God's bed. When Naomi finally settled down for a nap, Mary, talking more to herself than to her son or his new friend, said…

God's father, Jesus, made that bed… In that bed we made God … It is the bed of the greatest love this world has ever known… Sleep my child and peace attend thee… You have suffered enough… Now it is your turn to find love… Love… O love… To know I have known you… Jesus and Mary… Mary Magdalene and Jesus Christ… One… Take me now…

But she didn't die that day. Instead she slept.

TWENTY-ONE

God closed the door with nary a sound so as not to disturb Mary. They took a lonely path away from the town toward the River Jordan. Naomi had on some of Mary's clothes and a light scarf around her head.

You are lucky, God, to have a mother like that.

I know. No one chooses his or her parents. One must try to appreciate good ones and not let bad ones destroy you. That is your challenge, Naomi. It does no good to blame the world, especially parents. Good or bad, they allowed you to be in this world. One must make due with what one has, just like with one's legs, arms, heart, and mind.

I know. Of course I know. I have left my parents now. They will live their lives, and I will live mine.

Yes.

How far is it to the river? You don't think we're

taking a risk…

No. No more of a risk than staying in the house. If your father goes to every house in Nazareth, he'll come to ours. I don't think he'll go to a place by the river that he probably doesn't even know about. I have come here a hundred times and never met anybody.

When was the last time you bathed?

A week ago. And you?

Even longer. Maybe ten days. I'm glad you had the idea to go to the river.

And it's hot. The water will feel good on our bodies. Just be careful with your back.

It is feeling better since your mother put the ointment on it. I'll be fine. You know God, my father was so angry that I thought maybe he would kill me… and I thought that in so doing he might be doing me a favor.

God did not say anything. He tried to imagine what Naomi had been through and what it would have been like to have had a violent father. God had never experienced violence. The only pain he had had was from thinking about the suffering of others.

How much farther to the river?

Just a few minutes.

How did you find this path?

My mother showed me. She and Jesus would come to bathe away from the crowds. She and I came many times, but not recently… not since she has been feeling weak.

Do you fear she will die?
We all die.

They walked the rest of the way in silence. They undressed where Mary and Jesus had. When you love someone and they take off their clothes for the first time, it makes you love them even more. In love, everything fits.

TWENTY-TWO

Naomi would never know if her father had looked for her or not. They never saw each other again. He would do her no more harm. In any case, she would not stay in Judea much longer.

That evening, when God and Naomi came back from the river, Mary was up and putting food on the table. She had not worried when she awoke from her sleep and found them gone. She was too tired and weak to worry. Her only concern was setting out a few things to eat for when they got home. Darkness was near and she knew they would be there soon.

Mary sat with them at the table for a few minutes. They told her of their promenade to the river. No, they hadn't seen anybody. Yes, her back was feeling better. Yes, they had enough to eat. No, they didn't mind if she rested while they were still eating.

Mary lay down for the last time in God's bed. God and Naomi ate, talked softly, and put things away. They couldn't wait to get into the large bed in the corner of the room.

At the river they had held hands, embraced, and kissed a few times in the water. Then they dried, put their clothes back on and walked home. Now they took their clothes off for the night. Under the blanket – the same blanket Mary had had round her body at the foot of the cross on which Jesus died – God and Naomi caressed and kissed each other's body with the softest lips and the surest hands. They were both exactly where they wanted to be.

In the morning the world had a different Pietà. God held Mary's limp body in his arms. When God and Naomi finally finished crying, Naomi stayed in the house while God went out to find Joshua and Marcus. They helped him wrap his mother in her blanket, carry her to the olive grove, and bury her.

And yes, Mary died while God and Naomi were making love.

The next day the lovers quit Judea. There was nothing left for them in the holy land. Like Chaplin and Goddard at the end of *Modern Times*, arm in arm they wandered off to see the world, possessing nothing more than the clothes on their backs and their love for life and each other. God did have a few coins that he had saved from making shoes, but he gave them to a blind woman as they walked past Herod's temple.

ABOUT THE AUTHOR

Jon Ferguson was born in October 1949 in Oakland, California, into a
devout Christian family, much like his favorite philosopher, Friedrich
Nietzsche. In fact, as a child, church services were held in the family living
room. At age 17, his enthusiasm for sport was almost usurped by a
keenness to save the world when he enrolled at the Mormon-owned
Brigham Young University. Little by little, though, he realized that if Jesus
couldn't do it, neither could he. His faith in God began to crumble.
With an adieu to the US academic world where he'd been immersed
in anthropology and philosophy – and with a desire to engage with the
world at large – Ferguson hopped on a plane in 1973 and by chance ended
up in Nyon, Switzerland where he was soon playing basketball in the top
Swiss league, becoming a key player in what fans consider to have been
the golden age.
Half a century later, still in Switzerland, he is now just as well known for
his writing (eighteen books published in French) as for his coaching (thirty
years' worth). He won more games than any coach in Swiss basketball
history, but he likes to remind people that he lost more than everyone else
as well... He has written over twenty novels and a book on Nietzsche,
Nietzsche au Petit Déjeuner ("Nietzsche for Breakfast") and a book on the
history of Swiss basketball, Of Hoops and Men. For twenty-five years he
also wrote a bi-weekly column in the Lausanne newspaper called "Ainsi
Parla Schmaltz". His novel Farley's Jewel (Cinco Puntos Press, 1998) won a
Barnes & Noble "Discover Great New Writers of America" prize.
Find out more:
www.jonferguson.com

BOOKS BY JON FERGUSON

(Published by Huge Jam, 2022)

Adam's Cane
Foster's Depression
The Last Day Forever
Jesus & Mary
Mary & God
God & Naomi

Download 'The Last Day Forever' for free from the author's website
www.jonfergusonbooks.com

Out soon by the same author:

The Old Man and the Stone
Farmer's Daughter
Don't Bullshit Me Daddy
The Anthropologist

www.hugejam.com
www.jonfergusonbooks.com

www.ingramcontent.com/pod-product-compliance
Lightning Source LLC
Chambersburg PA
CBHW030842200726
48285CB00007B/2519

9 781911 249870